Dedicated to my mum, who always has
treasures in her pockets — L.M.

For Georgina, my little adventurous friend who has
plenty of need for a dress with pockets! — J.L.

Published by
PEACHTREE PUBLISHING COMPANY INC.
1700 Chattahoochee Avenue
Atlanta, Georgia 30318-2112
PeachtreeBooks.com

Text © 2022 by Lily Murray
Illustrations © 2022 by Jennie Løvlie

First published in Great Britain in 2022 by Macmillan Children's Books, an imprint of Pan Macmillan.
First United States version published in 2022 by Peachtree Publishing Company Inc.

The illustrations were rendered digitally.

Printed and bound in September 2022 in China.
10 9 8 7 6 5 4 3 2 1
First Edition
ISBN: 978-1-68263-533-9

Cataloging-in-Publication Data is available from the Library of Congress.

Lily Murray Jenny Løvlie

A DRESS WITH POCKETS

PEACHTREE
ATLANTA

On Lucy's birthday,
Aunt Augusta said,

"It's time you had
a new dress! I'll take
you shopping."

So off they went.

"Welcome!" said the shopkeeper. "At the Fabulous Fashion Store, we have every kind of dress and more! There are ...

... fancy dresses, frilly dresses, stripy dresses, silly dresses,

Sundresses,
fun dresses,
blue dresses,
green.

Swishy dresses, witchy dresses,

Very, very itchy dresses!

Swirly-twirly-whirly
dresses, fit for a queen.

"Furry dresses, feather dresses,
lacy dresses, leather dresses,

Headdresses, red dresses,
quiet dresses, LOUD!

Fairy dresses,
hairy dresses,

Watch out for
the scary dresses!

Wispy-gauzy-floaty dresses
for looking like a **cloud**!

"How about these puffy dresses?
Lovely pink and fluffy dresses!
Shiny dresses, spiny dresses, loose dresses . . .

...TIGHT!

Tied-up-in-a-knotty dresses,
polka-dotted spotty dresses,
slinky dresses, twinkly dresses,
lit up like the night!"

"Well?" asked Aunt Augusta.
"I don't know," said Lucy.
"None of these dresses feel quite . . . right."

"Not quite right?"

"Not quite right?"

"Not quite **right?**"

"What kind of dress *would* you like?"

And Lucy whispered,
"A dress with pockets."

"With pockets?"

"With pockets?"

"With pockets?
Whatever for?"

"Oh . . . ," sighed Lucy.

"For worms that wriggle and spiders that jiggle,

For beetles that live under logs!

For splashing in puddles, and giving wet cuddles

To beautiful, shiny green frogs.

"For magical spells
and beautiful shells,
for a wood louse,
a feather, a nest.

For following trails
and hunting for snails,

For a mouse in
need of a rest."

The shopkeeper spluttered, and turned rather pink.

"Dear me! Good gracious! The shock!
Never before have I heard such requests
when it comes to choosing a frock."

Lucy was quiet. She looked at the floor.
"I really need pockets, to help me . . .

"...EXPLORE!

For fossils and flints
for marbles and mints,
for trinkets and biscuits
and more.

For small sticky bricks, and lollipop sticks!
For a necklace, a bracelet, for rings.
For skipping stones and mysterious bones,
for a world of curious things!

"I don't care about spots
or blue polka-dots,

Or if it's made
with silken seams.

The dress that's the best is a dress
WITH POCKETS!
That is the dress of my dreams!"

The shopkeeper frowned and thought very hard.
"I think I may have just the thing!"

He rustled and rummaged,
then pulled from a corner
a box that was tied up with string.

"I've got it!

I've got it!

I've got it!

Yes! This is the dress for you!"

"Perfect," said Aunt Augusta . . .

. . . And they
took
two!

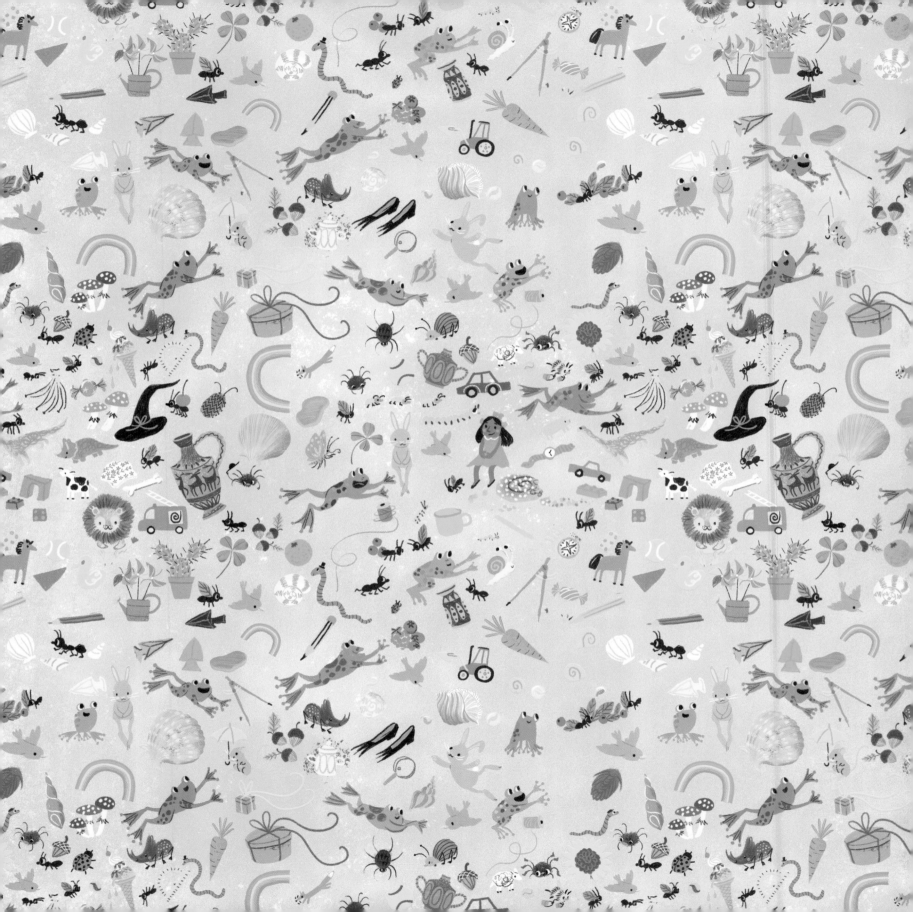